POPSUGAR

YOU'VE GOT THIS!

BY JESSICA MACLEISH

BY

LISA ... ... EINHART

THIS BOOK BELONGS TO _____

HI!

WELCOME TO *POPSUGAR: YOU'VE GOT THIS!*, A SUPER FUN ACTIVITY BOOK JUST FOR YOU! THESE PAGES WILL TAKE YOU THROUGH SOME OF THE ISSUES, QUESTIONS, AND TOPICS THAT ARE MOST IMPORTANT IN YOUR LIFE RIGHT NOW. WHAT MAKES YOU HAPPY? FRIENDS—LET'S CHAT ABOUT IT. CONFIDENCE—LET'S BUILD IT! BALANCE—LET'S FIND IT!

IF YOU'VE EVER WANTED TO GUSH ABOUT YOUR SECRET CRUSH, BRAINSTORM WAYS TO GET WHAT YOU WANT, KEEP YOUR COOL, EXPRESS YOURSELF, OR JUST CHANNEL GOOD VIBES OVERALL, THEN THIS BOOK IS FOR YOU!

THINK OF THESE PAGES AS A WAY TO LET IT ALL OUT AND ALSO INSPIRE YOU TO LEARN ABOUT YOURSELF. WHETHER YOU BLOW THROUGH THIS BOOK IN ONE SITTING OR COME BACK TO IT OVER AND OVER AGAIN, WE'RE HERE TO HELP YOU EXPRESS YOURSELF.

READY? LET'S DO THIS!

HAVE FUN! **XOXO, POPSUGAR**

LET'S KICK THINGS OFF BY GETTING DOWN TO BASICS. **WHAT MAKES YOU HAPPY?** USE THIS SPACE TO LIST ALL THE THINGS YOU CAN THINK OF THAT MAKE YOU SMILE, LAUGH, OR BRING YOU **JOY**—BIG OR SMALL.

TO HELP YOU GET STARTED, RATE THESE THINGS ON A SCALE OF ONE TO TEN SMILEY FACES ACCORDING TO HOW HAPPY THEY MAKE YOU (COLOR IN THE SMILEYS BASED ON YOUR MOOD—COLORING IN ALL TEN FACES MEANS THAT YOU ARE SUPER HAPPY!):

MY FAMILY: ☺ ☺ ☺ ☺ ☺ ☺ ☺ ☺ ☺ ☺

MY FRIENDS: ☺ ☺ ☺ ☺ ☺ ☺ ☺ ☺ ☺ ☺

LEARNING NEW THINGS: ☺ ☺ ☺ ☺ ☺ ☺ ☺ ☺ ☺ ☺

HELPING OTHER PEOPLE: ☺ ☺ ☺ ☺ ☺ ☺ ☺ ☺ ☺ ☺

ANIMALS: ☺ ☺ ☺ ☺ ☺ ☺ ☺ ☺ ☺ ☺

HOBBIES: ☺ ☺ ☺ ☺ ☺ ☺ ☺ ☺ ☺ ☺

SPORTS AND FITNESS: ☺ ☺ ☺ ☺ ☺ ☺ ☺ ☺ ☺ ☺

READING BOOKS: ☺ ☺ ☺ ☺ ☺ ☺ ☺ ☺ ☺ ☺

PLAYING VIDEO GAMES: ☺ ☺ ☺ ☺ ☺ ☺ ☺ ☺ ☺ ☺

PICK ONE THING FROM YOUR **HAPPINESS LIST** AND DRAW IT HERE! REMEMBER, ONCE IT'S ON THIS PAGE, YOU CAN ALWAYS COME BACK AND VISIT IT FOR A SMILE.

OKAY, SO THAT'S **YOUR** HAPPINESS—LET'S TALK ABOUT OTHER PEOPLE'S HAPPINESSES. CAN YOU THINK OF A TIME WHEN YOU MADE SOMEONE ELSE FEEL GOOD? DESCRIBE IT HERE. HOW DID IT MAKE THE OTHER PERSON (OR PEOPLE) FEEL? HOW DID IT MAKE YOU FEEL?

LIST FIVE THINGS YOU DID IN THE PAST MONTH TO HELP SOMEONE ELSE.

1 _____
_____

_____
_____ 2

3 _____
_____

_____
_____ 4

5 _____
_____

HAPPINESS IS CONTAGIOUS! MAKING OTHER PEOPLE HAPPY CAN MAKE **YOU** FEEL BETTER, TOO. WHAT ARE SOME WAYS THAT YOU CAN SPREAD HAPPINESS TO OTHERS—FAMILY OR FRIENDS OR STRANGERS—EVERY DAY? GOOD DEEDS CAN BE BIG OR SMALL: YOU COULD HELP A FAMILY MEMBER WITH CHORES OR HELP A FRIEND WITH THEIR HOMEWORK OR HELP YOUR COMMUNITY BY DONATING GOODS, VOLUNTEERING AT A FOOD BANK, OR PARTICIPATING IN A PARK CLEANUP!

USE THIS SPACE TO THINK OF SOME GOOD THINGS YOU CAN DO, BIG AND SMALL!

"FOR ME, **AS LONG AS MY FAMILY'S HAPPY,** I'M HAPPY."

—NAOMI OSAKA

OF COURSE, NO ONE IS 100% HAPPY 100% OF THE TIME.

MAYBE YOU'RE NOT FEELING SO AWESOME RIGHT NOW, AND THAT'S TOTALLY OKAY. YOU DON'T HAVE TO FIGHT YOUR EMOTIONS!

IT'S NORMAL TO FEEL SAD, ANGRY, OR ANXIOUS, OR LIKE THINGS ARE NOT GOING YOUR WAY AT ALL. WRITE ABOUT SOME OF THOSE LESS-THAN-HAPPY FEELINGS HERE: WHAT THEY ARE, HOW THEY FEEL, AND EXAMPLES OF WHEN YOU MIGHT FEEL THEM (LIKE BEFORE A BIG TEST OR IF YOU HAVE A FIGHT WITH A FRIEND OR SIBLING).

TIME TO BRAINSTORM! WHAT ARE SOME WAYS THAT YOU CAN GET YOURSELF OUT OF A FUNK OR SMILE AGAIN ONCE YOUR ANGER/SADNESS/WORRY/ETC. HAS PASSED?

HERE ARE SOME EXAMPLES TO GET YOU STARTED:

* CALL YOUR BFF.
* CREATE SOME TIKTOKS.
* BLAST YOUR FAVORITE SONG ON REPEAT.
*
*
*
*
*
*
*
*
*
*
*

* GET CRAFTY!
* BAKE SOMETHING SWEET!
* TAKE A WALK TO MOVE YOUR BODY.
*
*
*
*
*
*
*
*
*
*
*

A PART OF HAPPINESS IS LEARNING TO CELEBRATE THE GOOD THINGS, BIG AND SMALL. WHAT ARE SOME GOOD THINGS THAT HAVE HAPPENED IN YOUR LIFE LATELY? HOW DID YOU CELEBRATE THEM?

HERE ARE SOME EXAMPLES OF THINGS WE LOVE THAT ARE WORTH CELEBRATING:

Big

- ♥ GETTING A GOOD GRADE ON A TEST.
- ♥ A FAMILY VACATION.
- ♥ MAKING A NEW FRIEND.
- ♥
- ♥
- ♥
- ♥
- ♥
- ♥
- ♥

Small

- ✳ AN ICE—CREAM SUNDAE.
- ✳ A SLEEPOVER WITH FRIENDS.
- ✳
- ✳
- ✳
- ✳
- ✳
- ✳
- ✳
- ✳
- ✳
- ✳

WHAT IS MINDFULNESS, EXACTLY?

IT'S A STATE OF MIND ACHIEVED BY FOCUSING ON AWARENESS OF THE PRESENT AND ACCEPTING YOUR FEELINGS IN A GIVEN MOMENT. IT CAN BE CALMING AND FREEING, WHICH CAN LEAD TO FEELINGS OF HAPPINESS!

LET'S PRACTICE MINDFULNESS. TRY THIS SQUARE BREATHING TECHNIQUE:

♥ BEGIN BY SLOWLY EXHALING ALL OF YOUR AIR OUT.

♥ THEN, GENTLY INHALE THROUGH YOUR NOSE TO A SLOW COUNT OF 4.

♥ HOLD AT THE TOP OF THE BREATH FOR A COUNT OF 4.

♥ THEN, GENTLY EXHALE THROUGH YOUR MOUTH FOR A COUNT OF 4.

♥ AT THE BOTTOM OF THE BREATH, PAUSE AND HOLD FOR A COUNT OF 4.

HOW DID THAT FEEL? DID YOU FEEL MORE AWARE OF THE PRESENT MOMENT, YOUR FEELINGS, AND THOUGHTS? WRITE ABOUT IT OR DRAW A PICTURE; YOU DO YOU!

STOP! REWIND!

FLIP BACK TO THE PAGE WHERE YOU LISTED OUT ALL THE THINGS THAT MAKE YOU HAPPY. HOW CAN YOU MAKE SURE SOME OF THESE THINGS HAPPEN IN YOUR EVERYDAY LIFE? DREAM IT; DO IT!

WHICH THINGS WOULD WORK AS EVERYDAY HAPPINESSES, AND WHICH ARE BETTER LEFT FOR ONCE-IN-A-WHILE, SPECIAL-OCCASION HAPPINESSES? FOR EXAMPLE, YOU CAN'T TAKE A BIG VACATION OR CELEBRATE YOUR BIRTHDAY EVERY SINGLE DAY, BUT YOU CAN MAKE SURE YOU HUG YOUR BFF OR DO A HAPPY DANCE EVERY DAY OF THE WEEK. IT'S UP TO YOU!

"BEING HAPPY ISN'T HAVING EVERYTHING IN YOUR LIFE BE PERFECT. MAYBE IT'S ABOUT STRINGING TOGETHER ALL THE LITTLE THINGS."
—ANN BRASHARES, *THE SISTERHOOD OF THE TRAVELING PANTS*

WE'VE TALKED A LOT ABOUT HOW **YOU** CAN MAKE YOU HAPPY—BUT WHAT ARE SOME WAYS YOU GAIN HAPPINESS FROM OTHERS? HOW DO THE PEOPLE AROUND YOU CONTRIBUTE TO YOUR HAPPINESS?

FILL IN THIS BLANK BINGO CARD WITH SOME OF THE WAYS YOU MAKE YOURSELF HAPPY AND THE WAYS OTHERS MAKE YOU FEEL GOOD.

TRY TO GET HAPPY EVERY WEEK FOR A MONTH!

USE A DIFFERENT COLOR PEN TO MARK BOXES OFF EACH WEEK, SO YOU CAN KEEP THINGS STRAIGHT.

SURPRISE!

DID YOU KNOW THAT A SURPRISE CAN MAKE YOU FEEL BOTH PSYCHED AND ANXIOUS? AND THAT'S OKAY!

WHEN WAS THE LAST TIME YOU WERE TRULY SHOCKED—BY A SURPRISE SOMEONE PLANNED FOR YOU, BY SURPRISINGLY LIKING A NEW ACTIVITY OR FOOD, OR SOMETHING ELSE? DESCRIBE THE SITUATION AND HOW IT FELT:

WHAT ARE SOME WAYS YOU CAN INTRODUCE SURPRISE INTO YOUR LIFE ON THE REG? LIST SOME IDEAS ON THIS PAGE.

SOME SUGGESTIONS TO START YOU OFF:

* TRY A NEW FOOD.
* SPONTANEOUS DANCE PARTIES!
* LEARN A NEW WORD EVERY DAY.
* TRY A NEW SPORT.
* TAKE A SELFIE IN THE SAME PLACE, SAME TIME EVERY DAY.
*
*
*
*
*
*
*
*

*
*
*
*
*
*
*
*
*
*
*
*
*

NOW IT'S TIME TO GET INSPIRED. ASK FIVE PEOPLE WHAT MAKES THEM HAPPY AND RECORD THEIR ANSWERS HERE—WHAT DO YOU HAVE IN COMMON? WHICH OF THESE MOTIVATED YOU TO TRY TO DISCOVER HAPPINESS IN NEW WAYS?

1 _____
   _____

   _____ 2
   _____

3 _____
   _____

   _____ 4
   _____

5 _____
   _____

"SPEND LESS TIME TEARING YOURSELF APART, WORRYING IF YOU'RE GOOD ENOUGH. **YOU ARE GOOD ENOUGH.** AND YOU'RE GOING TO MEET AMAZING PEOPLE IN YOUR LIFE WHO WILL HELP YOU AND **LOVE YOU.**"

—REESE WITHERSPOON

NOW CREATE YOUR OWN HAPPINESS MOOD BOARD WITH YOUR FAVORITE QUOTES, SONG LYRICS, EMOJI, AND DOODLES.

FILL IN THIS PAGE WITH YOUR CURRENT FAVORITE HAPPY COLORS! CUT IT OUT. HANG IT UP ON YOUR WALL OR IN YOUR LOCKER, OR GIVE IT TO A FRIEND.

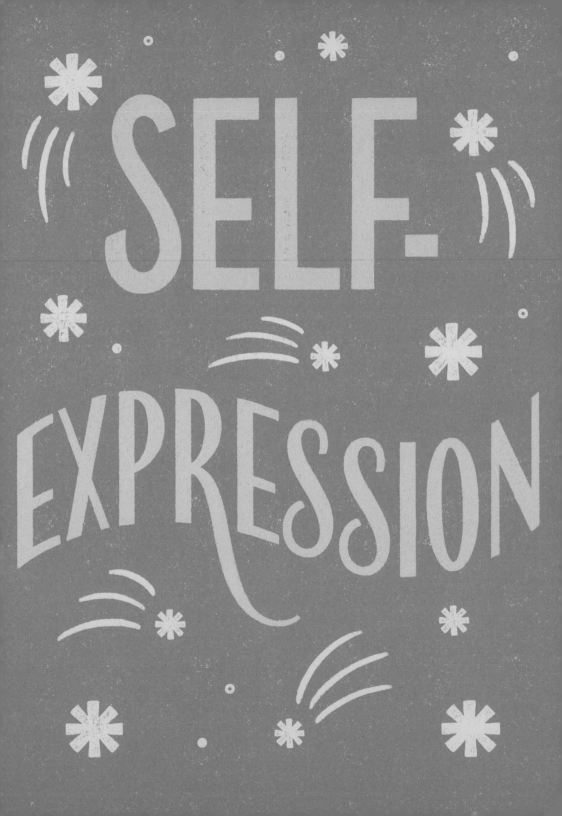

SELFIE TIME!

HOW CAN YOU EXPRESS YOURSELF ARTISTICALLY? USE THIS PAGE TO DRAW A SELF-PORTRAIT THAT CAPTURES WHAT MAKES YOU YOU! THIS COULD INCLUDE YOUR APPEARANCE, YOUR FAVORITE OUTFIT, NAIL ART, HAIRSTYLE, AND ACCESSORIES, OR IT COULD BE A TOTALLY RANDOM DRAWING OF WHAT MAKES YOU UNIQUE.

"I PROMISE YOU THAT EACH AND EVERY ONE OF YOU IS **MADE TO BE WHO YOU ARE** AND THAT'S WHAT'S SO ATTRACTIVE AND **BEAUTIFUL.**"

—SELENA GOMEZ

HOW CAN YOU EXPRESS YOURSELF THROUGH WRITING? **USE THIS PAGE TO WRITE A PROFILE OF YOURSELF AS IF YOU WERE A CHARACTER IN A BOOK, MOVIE, TV SHOW, OR PLAY. DESCRIBE YOUR BACKGROUND, SPECIAL SKILLS, APPEARANCE, LIKES/DISLIKES, AND PERSONALITY!**

IT CAN BE HARD TO EXPRESS YOUR THOUGHTS AND FEELINGS, ESPECIALLY WHEN YOU'RE UPSET! **CAN YOU REMEMBER A TIME WHEN YOU WISH YOU'D EXPRESSED YOURSELF BETTER? DESCRIBE IT HERE. WHAT COULD YOU DO DIFFERENTLY NEXT TIME YOU ARE IN A SIMILAR SITUATION?**

ON THE FLIP SIDE, YOU MIGHT BE REALLY GOOD AT EXPRESSING YOUR FEELINGS AND THOUGHTS. **DESCRIBE A TIME WHEN YOU WERE REALLY PROUD OF HOW YOU EXPRESSED YOURSELF. HOW DID IT FEEL? HOW CAN YOU CHANNEL THAT MEMORY THE NEXT TIME YOU NEED TO SHARE SOMETHING?**

_____

_____

_____

_____

_____

_____

_____

_____

_____

"EVERYONE LOOKS TO AN ARTIST FOR SOMETHING MORE THAN JUST THE MUSIC, AND THAT **MESSAGE OF BEING COMFORTABLE IN MY OWN SKIN IS NUMBER ONE** FOR ME."

—LIZZO

THERE ARE SO MANY WAYS TO SHOW OFF YOUR PERSONALITY, AND ONE OF THE MOST FUN IS THROUGH MUSIC.

TRY TO THINK OF SOME OF YOUR FAVORITE SONGS RELATED TO THE EMOTIONS BELOW.

HOW DOES EACH OF YOUR SONGS EXPRESS THOSE FEELINGS? IS IT THE BEAT, LYRICS, OR OVERALL VIBE? YOU DECIDE!

HAPPINESS:

SADNESS:

LOVE:

ANGER:

HURT FEELINGS:

ARE THERE MORE YOU CAN THINK OF? LIST THEM HERE:

"PEOPLE HAVEN'T ALWAYS BEEN THERE FOR ME BUT **MUSIC ALWAYS HAS.**"
—TAYLOR SWIFT

LOOK AT YOUR LAST FIVE POSTS ON YOUR FAVORITE SOCIAL MEDIA PLATFORM. ANSWER THESE QUESTIONS ABOUT EACH ONE TO GET A SENSE OF HOW WELL YOU'RE USING SOCIAL MEDIA TO EXPRESS YOURSELF!

1 IS IT HONEST AND AUTHENTIC?

_____

_____

2 DOES IT REPRESENT YOU?

_____

_____

3 WHAT DO YOU LIKE ABOUT IT?

_____

_____

4 WHY DID YOU POST IT?

_____

_____

5 HOW COULD YOU MAKE YOUR SOCIAL POSTS A BETTER REPRESENTATION OF YOU?

_____

_____

_____

_____

EXPRESSING YOURSELF SOMETIMES MEANS STANDING UP FOR YOURSELF, OTHERS, AND WHAT YOU BELIEVE IN! LIST FIVE THINGS YOU BELIEVE IN HERE—THESE COULD BE MORALS, VALUES, OR RELIGIOUS BELIEFS.

NEXT TO EACH ONE, WRITE OUT AN IDEA FOR HOW YOU CAN STAND UP FOR THOSE BELIEFS. YOU ARE CREATING YOUR OWN CREED.

HERE'S AN EXAMPLE TO KICK THINGS OFF: I BELIEVE THAT EVERYONE SHOULD BE TREATED THE SAME! EQUAL RIGHTS FOR ALL!

1 _____

2 _____

3 _____

4 _____

5 _____

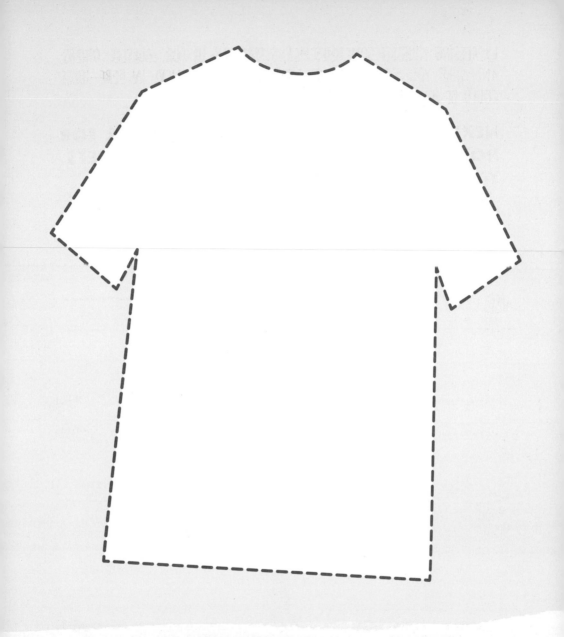

MAKE UP A T-SHIRT SLOGAN THAT SHOWS OFF ONE OF YOUR BELIEFS OR VALUES, AND DESIGN YOUR VERY OWN T-SHIRT HERE!

Quiz Time

WHAT EMOJI REPRESENTS YOUR PERSONALITY THE BEST? ANSWER THE QUESTIONS BELOW TO FIND OUT!

WHEN YOU'RE HAPPY, YOU . . .

A: DO A SPECIAL HAPPY DANCE!

B: WRITE ABOUT YOUR FEELINGS IN YOUR DIARY.

C: CALL ALL YOUR FRIENDS AND SPREAD HAPPY VIBES.

WHEN YOU'RE SAD, YOU . . .

A: SING ALONG TO A SAD SONG, EVEN IF YOU DON'T KNOW ALL THE LYRICS.

B: WRITE A POEM.

C: TELL EVERYONE AROUND YOU HOW YOU'RE FEELING AND WHY.

YOU DESCRIBE YOURSELF AS . . .

A: QUIRKY

B: SHY AND THOUGHTFUL

C: THE LIFE OF THE PARTY

YOU LOVE TO . . .

A: EXPRESS YOURSELF THROUGH YOUR CREATIVE STYLE.

B: READ IN THE PARK.

C: TELL JOKES THAT MAKE EVERYONE LAUGH.

RESULTS:

MOSTLY As: YOU'RE THE ALIEN EMOJI—TOTALLY, UNIQUELY YOU!

MOSTLY Bs: YOU'RE THE CATERPILLAR EMOJI—A TOTAL BOOKWORM!

MOSTLY Cs: YOU'RE THE PARTY HORN EMOJI—BOLD AND FUN-LOVING!

STOP WHATEVER YOU'RE DOING AND GIVE YOURSELF A COMPLIMENT, RIGHT HERE, RIGHT NOW:

NOW ANOTHER ONE:

NOW ANOTHER ONE:

NOW TAKE THOSE THREE COMPLIMENTS AND USE THEM TO CREATE A CONFIDENCE CHEER FOR YOURSELF! WORKSHOP IT ON THIS PAGE:

THIS IS THE CHEER TO REPEAT WHEN YOU'RE FEELING DOWN ON YOURSELF. (REMEMBER: YOU'RE AWESOME! YOU TOLD YOURSELF SO ON THE PREVIOUS PAGE.)

"AM I GOOD ENOUGH? YES I AM."
—MICHELLE OBAMA, *BECOMING*

NEVER FORGET THAT YOU SHOULD BE YOUR #1 FAN!

WHAT ARE SOME PERSONAL CHEERS YOU CAN USE TO PUMP YOURSELF UP DURING GOOD AND BAD SITUATIONS? BRAINSTORM HERE.

HERE'S AN EXAMPLE: TRY SPELLING OUT YOUR NAME IN A CHANT, AND THEN COMING UP WITH A FEW SHORT RHYMING LINES ABOUT HOW GREAT YOU ARE!

_____

_____

_____

_____

_____

_____

_____

_____

_____

_____

_____

"DON'T TRY SO HARD TO FIT IN, AND CERTAINLY DON'T TRY SO HARD TO BE DIFFERENT . . . JUST TRY HARD TO BE YOU."
—ZENDAYA

NOW USE THIS SPACE TO WRITE A LETTER TO YOURSELF, CHEERING YOU ON—ABOUT ANYTHING YOU WANT!

CONFIDENCE CAN COME FROM BOTH THE INSIDE AND OUT!

WHAT'S AN OUTFIT OR HAIRSTYLE THAT MAKES YOU FEEL BOLD? HOW ELSE DOES IT MAKE YOU FEEL? GET DESCRIPTIVE AND THEN DRAW YOURSELF IN YOUR POWER OUTFIT/HAIRSTYLE HERE.

THIS IS YOUR OFFICIAL CONFIDENCE SUPERHERO UNIFORM! WHAT'S YOUR SUPERHERO NAME, AND WHAT SUPERPOWERS WOULD YOU HAVE? THERE ARE NO WRONG ANSWERS—WHATEVER YOU COME UP WITH IS SURE TO BE AWESOME.

_____

_____

_____

OKAY, IT'S TIME TO LOOK INTO THE CRYSTAL BALL AND SEE WHAT THE FUTURE HOLDS! OR AT LEAST WHAT YOU **HOPE** IT HOLDS. **WHAT ARE SOME THINGS YOU HOPE TO ACHIEVE IN THE NEXT THREE MONTHS?**

. . . IN THE NEXT SIX MONTHS?

. . . HOW ABOUT IN THE NEXT YEAR?

YOU CAN ACHIEVE ALMOST ANYTHING WITH THE RIGHT AMOUNT OF CONFIDENCE. WHAT ARE SOME STEPS YOU CAN TAKE TO MAKE SURE THIS FUTURE VISION BECOMES REALITY? DON'T FORGET TO CHECK OFF OR CROSS OUT EACH STEP AS YOU ACCOMPLISH IT, AND TURN BACK TO THIS PAGE OFTEN TO MAKE SURE YOU'RE ON TRACK (OR TO CHANGE YOUR GOALS—THAT'S FINE, TOO!).

EMBARRASSMENT CAN BE ONE OF CONFIDENCE'S WORST ENEMIES. WHEN WE FEEL EMBARRASSED, WE OFTEN DON'T FEEL OUR BRIGHTEST AND BOLDEST. AND THAT'S OKAY! EVERYONE FEELS LIKE THAT SOMETIMES—YOU'RE NOT ALONE. THINK OF AN EMBARRASSING MEMORY, AND THEN REWRITE HISTORY HERE. WHAT WOULD YOU CHANGE ABOUT IT IF YOU COULD?

_____

_____

_____

_____

_____

_____

_____

_____

_____

_____

_____

WE HAVE THE POWER TO MOVE ON AND THE POWER TO LAUGH AT OURSELVES. WHAT FEELS LIKE A HORRIFYING AND EMBARRASSING MOMENT NOW WILL MOST LIKELY BE A LONG-LOST MEMORY ONE DAY!

ANOTHER ENEMY OF CONFIDENCE IS DOUBT. EVERYONE EXPERIENCES A LITTLE SELF-DOUBT—REALLY, EVERYONE. WHAT ARE SOME DOUBTS YOU HAVE ABOUT YOURSELF OR YOUR SKILLS? IS IT POSSIBLE TO OVERCOME THESE DOUBTS?

FILL OUT THE CHART BELOW WITH SOME OF YOUR DOUBTS IN THE LEFT COLUMN, AND IDEAS FOR HOW TO VANQUISH THOSE DOUBTS IN THE RIGHT COLUMN.

AN EXAMPLE OF SELF-DOUBT MIGHT BE GETTING NERVOUS BEFORE READING ALOUD TO YOUR ENTIRE CLASS. A SOLUTION TO THAT WOULD BE PRACTICING READING OUT LOUD WHEN YOU'RE ALONE SO THAT YOU ARE MUCH MORE COMFORTABLE WHEN YOU HAVE TO DO IT IN FRONT OF OTHERS.

SELF-DOUBTS	SOLUTIONS

REMEMBER THAT YOU CAN DO ANYTHING IF YOU SET YOUR MIND TO IT, AND THAT YOU CAN **ALWAYS** ASK FOR HELP IF YOU NEED IT.

"I WAS MADE **EXACTLY** THE WAY I WAS MEANT TO BE MADE IN **WHO I AM** AND MY PERSONALITY AND THE WAY I WAS BORN."

—MEGAN RAPINOE

COLOR IN THE ICONS BELOW—JUST FOR FUN!

SO WE KNOW WHAT YOU'RE GOOD AT—AND P.S.: YOU ARE TOTALLY IMPRESSIVE. BUT WHAT DO YOU WANT TO GET BETTER AT? **LIST FIVE SKILLS YOU'D LIKE TO LEARN FROM SCRATCH OR GET BETTER AT HERE, AS WELL AS HOW YOU CAN ACHIEVE EACH ONE.**

SOME SUGGESTIONS, IN CASE YOU HAVE A BRAINSTORM BLOCK:

* LEARN TO BAKE A CAKE (WHATEVER YOUR FAVORITE IS!).

* LEARN ALL ABOUT SOMETHING YOU'VE ALWAYS BEEN INTERESTED IN.

* RAISE YOUR HAND IN CLASS MORE OFTEN.

* SCORE MORE GOALS.

1 _____

_____

_____ **2**

_____

3 _____

_____

_____ **4**

_____

5 _____

_____

"WHEN YOU HAVE CONFIDENCE, YOU CAN DO ANYTHING."

—SLOANE STEPHENS

Quiz Time

SELECT THE ANSWERS THAT BEST APPLY TO YOU BELOW TO DETERMINE YOUR CONFIDENCE LEVEL AND STYLE:

WHEN YOU FEEL DOWN ON YOURSELF, WHAT DO YOU DO TO LIFT YOUR SPIRITS BACK UP AGAIN?

A: I MOPE ABOUT IT UNTIL SOMEONE ELSE REMINDS ME HOW GREAT I AM.

B: I GIVE MYSELF THE PEP TALK THAT I'VE PREPARED AND MEMORIZED FOR JUST SUCH OCCASIONS!

C: I VENT ABOUT MY FEELINGS THROUGH WRITING OR ARTWORK.

YOU KNOW YOU'RE AWESOME. HOW DO YOU SHOUT IT OUT TO THE WORLD?

A: I WAIT FOR OTHERS TO RECOGNIZE MY SKILLS AND GIVE ME PRAISE OR AN AWARD.

B: I TELL EVERYONE, LOUD AND PROUD, HOW GREAT I AM!

C: I MOVE THROUGH MY DAY KNOWING I CAN HANDLE ANYTHING THAT COMES MY WAY.

WHERE DOES YOUR CONFIDENCE COME FROM?

A: THE COMPLIMENTS FROM THOSE AROUND ME.

B: THE KNOWLEDGE THAT I'M AWESOME: ALWAYS HAVE BEEN AND ALWAYS WILL BE!

C: THE FACT THAT I'M GOOD AT WHAT I'M GOOD AT, AND GOOD AT KNOWING WHEN I NEED HELP OR COULD IMPROVE, TOO.

RESULTS:

MOSTLY As: YOUR CONFIDENCE MOSTLY COMES FROM EXTERNAL VALIDATION—AND WHO DOESN'T LIKE GETTING COMPLIMENTS OR PRAISE? BUT REMEMBER THAT CONFIDENCE CAN COME FROM WITHIN YOURSELF, TOO!

MOSTLY Bs: YOU FEEL 100% CONFIDENT, 100% OF THE TIME, AND YOU MAKE SURE THE WORLD KNOWS IT!

MOSTLY Cs: YOU HAVE A HEALTHY BALANCE OF CONFIDENCE AND KNOW THAT THERE'S ALWAYS ROOM TO GET BETTER AT SOMETHING.

BALANCE

STRESS—EVERYONE FEELS IT! BUT DIFFERENT THINGS CAN CAUSE STRESS OR ANXIETY IN EACH AND EVERY ONE OF US. **WHAT MAKES YOU STRESSED, ANXIOUS, OR WORRIED? DON'T HOLD BACK—LIST ALL THE THINGS, BIG AND LITTLE, LIKE STUDYING FOR A TEST OR FEAR OF TRYING A NEW ACTIVITY.**

"IT'S NOT ABOUT **PERFECTION**. IT'S ABOUT **PURPOSE**."

—BEYONCÉ

LOOKING AT A SOOTHING IMAGE CAN HELP CALM YOUR MIND DOWN WHEN YOU'RE FEELING ANXIOUS OR STRESSED. **CIRCLE THE EMOJI THAT YOU FIND MOST CALMING OR HAPPY, AND THEN DRAW A FEW OF YOUR OWN THAT WILL HELP SOOTHE YOU WHEN YOU NEED IT!**

SCRIBBLE TIME! USE THESE PAGES TO SCRIBBLE WHATEVER YOU WANT AND TO LET
OUT ANY ANGER, SADNESS, OR STRESS YOU MIGHT BE FEELING.

YOU COULD SCRAWL AS HARD AS YOU CAN TO EXPRESS YOUR FEELINGS, OR TRY DRAWING SOMETHING SIMPLE AND CALMING TO SOOTHE YOURSELF. (FOR EXAMPLE, DRAW LOTS AND LOTS OF CIRCLES OF ALL SHAPES AND SIZES, OR START IN THE CORNER AND DRAW TREE BRANCHES THAT GROW ACROSS THE PAGE.) WHATEVER YOU DO, DON'T STOP UNTIL THE PAGES ARE FILLED AND YOU FEEL A LITTLE BETTER!

Quiz Time

TRY THIS SHORT QUIZ TO HELP DETERMINE HOW YOU FEEL ABOUT KEEPING AN ORGANIZED TO-DO LIST AND SCHEDULE!

LOOKING AT A TO-DO LIST MAKES ME FEEL _____

A: OVERWHELMED ABOUT EVERYTHING I HAVE TO DO

B: READY TO GET TO WORK ASAP

C: CALM, LIKE I TOOK THE FIRST STEP IN STOPPING MY STRESS

WHEN MY DAYS ARE SCHEDULED DOWN TO THE MINUTE, I FEEL _____

A: TRAPPED, LIKE THERE'S NO ROOM FOR SURPRISE OR FLEXIBILITY

B: GREAT. I CAN'T FUNCTION IF MY DAY ISN'T TOTALLY SCHEDULED.

C: RELAXED BECAUSE I HAVE A PLAN FOR WHEN TO DO EVERYTHING ON MY TO-DO LIST, BUT I'M OKAY DEVIATING FROM THE SCHEDULE IF OTHER THINGS COME UP.

I TYPICALLY DO MY HOMEWORK _____

A: WHENEVER I HAVE THE TIME, AND SOMETIMES AT THE LAST MINUTE

B: AS SOON AS I GET HOME FROM SCHOOL, BEFORE DOING ANYTHING ELSE

C: AFTER SCHOOL, BUT I MAKE SURE TO TAKE BREAKS AND DO OTHER ACTIVITIES, TOO

RESULTS:

MOSTLY As: YOU'RE A FREE SPIRIT WHO DOESN'T WANT A LIST OR SCHEDULE TELLING YOU WHAT TO DO, BUT DON'T FORGET THAT SOMETIMES YOU'LL NEED TO BUCKLE DOWN AND GET THINGS DONE!

MOSTLY Bs: YOU NEED A REGIMENTED TO-DO LIST AND SCHEDULE TO KEEP YOURSELF ON TRACK AND WORRY-FREE, BUT DON'T FORGET TO TAKE DEEP BREATHS AND GIVE YOURSELF A BREAK SOMETIMES!

MOSTLY Cs: YOU LIKE A SCHEDULE AND A TO-DO LIST, BUT YOU ALSO BUILD IN TIME FOR FLEXIBILITY AND FUN! MAKE SURE YOU KEEP CHECKING IN WITH YOURSELF TO UNDERSTAND WHICH APPROACH IS BEST FOR YOU AT ANY GIVEN TIME.

A TO-DO LIST CAN BE A GOOD WAY TO KEEP YOURSELF ON TRACK, ESPECIALLY IF YOU HAVE A LOT OF HOMEWORK AND AFTER-SCHOOL ACTIVITIES TO KEEP STRAIGHT. BUT WHEN A TO-DO LIST BECOMES TOO LONG AND UNWIELDLY, IT CAN QUICKLY GET OVERWHELMING! TO MAKE (AND STICK TO) A FOCUSED TO-DO LIST, TRY BREAKING THE ITEMS INTO CATEGORIES. (LIKE GOALS FOR EACH DAY OF THE WEEK OR COLOR CODING FOR ACTIVITIES AND DEADLINES!)

TEST OUT YOUR NEW FOCUSED TO-DO LIST HERE!

CUT THIS PAGE OUT AND HANG IT SOMEWHERE YOU'LL SEE IT EVERY DAY, TO REMIND YOU TO PRESS PAUSE AND BREATHE!
TRY HANGING IT UP IN YOUR LOCKER AT SCHOOL OR YOUR BEDROOM WALL.

YOU MAY WANT A DIFFERENT CHEER TO REPEAT TO YOURSELF, IN CASE THE DEEP BREATHING REMINDER ISN'T ENOUGH. SO LET'S BRAINSTORM! WHAT ARE SOME THINGS THAT MAKE YOU FEEL CALM AND HAPPY? **LIST THEM ALL HERE AND THEN WORKSHOP A FEW DIFFERENT REMINDERS THAT COULD HELP YOU SOOTHE YOUR STRESS AND WORRY.**

HERE ARE A FEW EXAMPLES TO KICK YOU OFF:

REMEMBER: _____ LOVES YOU!

THE WORLD IS A BETTER PLACE BECAUSE _____,
_____, AND _____ EXIST.

THIS WILL PASS, AND THINKING ABOUT _____
(SOMETHING YOU'RE LOOKING FORWARD TO) WILL HELP IT PASS FASTER!

WHEN THINGS GET STRESSFUL, COUNT TO _____ (YOUR LUCKY NUMBER) AND PICTURE _____ (YOUR FAVORITE PLACE).

_____

_____

_____

_____

_____

_____

_____

LUCKY YOU, YOU CAN CONNECT WITH FRIENDS INSTANTLY AND FIND INFORMATION AT RAPID SPEEDS THANKS TO THE DEVICES YOU HAVE IN YOUR HOME. SOMETIMES SCREEN TIME IS THE BEST, BUT IT CAN ALSO BE OVERWHELMING. DO YOU FIND YOURSELF GETTING HEADACHES, FEELING STRESSED, OR ADDICTED TO YOUR DEVICES?

SET ASIDE SOME "UNPLUGGING" TIME EACH NIGHT AND FOCUS ON AN OFFLINE HOBBY. WHAT ARE SOME HOBBIES YOU CAN DO THAT DON'T INVOLVE SCREENS? **MAKE A LIST HERE AND THEN MAKE A PLAN TO START YOUR FAVORITE ONE (OR TWO OR THREE)!**

"I COULD LIVE **WITHOUT MY PHONE.** AND ONE THING I'D LOVE TO DO IS EXPERIENCE **HAVING THE FREEDOM** THAT KIDS HAD BACK IN THE '80S."
—MILLIE BOBBY BROWN

SOCIAL MEDIA CAN BE A FUN WAY TO CONNECT WITH FRIENDS AND EXPRESS YOURSELF, BUT SPENDING TOO MUCH TIME ONLINE CAN BE STRESSFUL, TOO! **USE THIS GRAPHIC TO HELP CREATE YOUR IDEAL DAILY SCHEDULE—FILL IN BLUE FOR SCHOOL/HOMEWORK, GREEN FOR HANGING OUT WITH FRIENDS, ORANGE FOR FAMILY TIME, YELLOW FOR ENTERTAINMENT, AND RED FOR TIME SPENT ON SOCIAL MEDIA.** IF YOU SEE TOO MUCH RED, BRAINSTORM WAYS TO BALANCE OUT YOUR TIME. WHO WOULDN'T WANT TO SPEND MORE TIME WITH FRIENDS?!

MONDAY

TUESDAY

WEDNESDAY

THURSDAY

FRIDAY

SATURDAY

SUNDAY

ONE THING THAT CAN HELP REDUCE STRESS AND ANXIETY AND INCREASE WELL-BEING AND HAPPINESS IS TAKING GOOD CARE OF YOURSELF. IT'S NEVER TOO SOON TO START PRACTICING GOOD SELF-CARE HABITS. SELF-CARE CAN BE THINGS LIKE TAKING A BUBBLE BATH, MEDITATING, TALKING YOUR FEELINGS OUT, AND SO MUCH MORE! **WHAT ARE SOME THINGS YOU DO TO MAKE YOURSELF FEEL HAPPY AND HEALTHY?**

YOUR BEDROOM CAN BE YOUR SANCTUARY—A SPACE ALL YOUR OWN WHERE YOU CAN BE YOURSELF AND ENJOY YOUR OWN COMPANY! EVEN IF YOU SHARE YOUR ROOM, THERE'S BOUND TO BE A CORNER OR SPACE THAT YOU CAN CLAIM.

PICK A SPOT IN YOUR ROOM THAT YOU WANT TO MAKE YOUR CALM ZONE, A PLACE TO GO WHEN YOU'RE FEELING STRESSED AND JUST FOCUS ON BREATHING EXERCISES OR COLORING OR ANYTHING THAT SOOTHES YOU.

DRAW IT HERE, AND DON'T FORGET TO INCLUDE ALL THE DETAILS THAT MAKE IT THE PERFECT CALM ZONE.

PUMP YOURSELF UP! TIME FOR SOME POSITIVITY. WE ALL NEED A LITTLE PICK ME UP EVERY ONCE IN AWHILE. REPEAT THESE WORDS TO YOURSELF WHEN YOU ARE FEELING LESS THAN AWESOME:

YOU ARE ENOUGH.

ENJOY THE LITTLE THINGS.

CULTIVATE KINDNESS.

IT'S OK TO NOT BE OK.

WORK HARD. PLAY NICE.

POWER YOUR HAPPY

NOW LET'S TRY A CALMING EXERCISE, BECAUSE STRESS AND ANXIETY AFFECT BOTH THE MIND AND BODY. YOU CAN USE THIS WHENEVER YOU'RE FEELING TENSE OR STRESSED OUT. BE SURE TO MARK THIS PAGE SO YOU CAN FIND IT AGAIN IN A FEW DAYS, WEEKS, OR MONTHS.

LIE DOWN AND TENSE ALL OF YOUR MUSCLES, THEN START AT YOUR HEAD AND TRAVEL DOWN YOUR BODY, GRADUALLY RELAXING ALL THE MAJOR MUSCLES AS YOU GO. WHEN YOU'RE DONE, ALL OF YOUR MUSCLES WILL BE COMPLETELY RELAXED. YOU CAN ALSO DO THIS SITTING UP, LIKE IN CLASS BEFORE A TEST OR A PRESENTATION THAT HAS YOU FEELING NERVOUS.

HOW DO YOU FEEL AFTER TRYING THIS EXERCISE? **CIRCLE THE EMOJI THAT BEST REPRESENTS YOUR STATE OF MIND.**

REMEMBER SEESAWS FROM THE PLAYGROUND? A SEESAW IS ALSO A GREAT METAPHOR FOR BALANCE. **COLOR IN THE SEESAW IMAGES BELOW, AND THEN WRITE DOWN ALL THE THINGS YOU'RE BALANCING IN YOUR LIFE.** (ON TOP OF THE GROUNDED SEAT, WRITE THE THINGS YOU HAVE TO DO—LIKE HOMEWORK, CHORES, ETC.; ON TOP OF THE SEAT IN THE AIR, WRITE THE THINGS YOU CHOOSE TO DO—LIKE HANGING OUT WITH FRIENDS OR SPENDING TIME ON SOCIAL MEDIA.)

HOW COULD YOU BALANCE THESE THINGS MORE? **REWRITE THEM ON THE BALANCED SEESAW BELOW.**

IT'S NEVER A BAD TIME TO MAKE A NEW FRIEND! BUT HOW DO YOU DO IT? ONE WAY IS TO START WITH SOMETHING YOU AND YOUR POTENTIAL NEW BFF HAVE IN COMMON. BRAINSTORM A LIST OF ACTIVITIES AND PLACES THAT YOU LIKE WHERE YOU COULD MEET SOME NEW PEOPLE.

THINK BACK TO THE THINGS THAT MAKE YOU HAPPY, BECAUSE A HAPPY MOOD IS A GOOD PLACE TO START WHEN MAKING A FRIEND. FOR EXAMPLE, IF YOU LIKE TO SWIM, THE LOCAL POOL OR BEACH OR LAKE MIGHT BE A GOOD SPOT TO MEET OTHER WATER LOVERS!

* _____
* _____
* _____
* _____
* _____
* _____
* _____
* _____
* _____
* _____
* _____
* _____
* _____
* _____
* _____

NOW THINK UP SOME IDEAS FOR HOW TO START CHATTING WITH YOUR NEW FRIENDS. WHAT ARE SOME TOPICS YOU CAN MENTION?

HERE ARE A FEW TO START YOU OFF:

* ASK IF THEY GO TO SCHOOL IN THE AREA.

* COMPLIMENT SOMETHING THEY'RE WEARING OR A SKILL THEY HAVE THAT YOU'VE NOTICED.

LET'S TAKE A MOMENT TO CELEBRATE ALL YOUR BESTIES! WHO ARE YOUR CLOSEST FRIENDS (HUMAN OR ANIMAL!) AND WHAT DO YOU LOVE ABOUT THEM? **WRITE DOWN THEIR NAMES, DRAW A PICTURE THAT REPRESENTS THEM, AND WRITE YOUR THREE FAVORITE THINGS ABOUT THEM:**

"ANYTHING IS POSSIBLE WHEN YOU HAVE THE RIGHT PEOPLE THERE TO SUPPORT YOU."

—MISTY COPELAND

EVERY FRIENDSHIP GOES THROUGH ITS ROUGH PATCHES. IT'S NATURAL FOR FRIENDS TO DISAGREE OR SOMETIMES FIGHT. MOST OF THE TIME, YOU CAN FIND A WAY TO MAKE UP! **WHAT ARE SOME WAYS YOU COULD RESOLVE DIFFERENT ARGUMENTS? LIST THEM HERE AND REFER TO THE LIST THE NEXT TIME YOU AND A FRIEND AREN'T GETTING ALONG.**

DISAGREEMENTS

RESOLUTIONS

DISAGREEMENTS	RESOLUTIONS
YOU AND YOUR FRIEND CAN'T AGREE ON HOW TO WORK TOGETHER ON A SCHOOL PROJECT.	TRY FINDING A COMPROMISE THAT BLENDS BOTH OF YOUR IDEAS.
A FRIEND IS BULLYING YOU.	LET THEM KNOW THAT WHAT THEY ARE DOING (OR SAYING) IS HURTFUL.

P.S.: SOMETIMES PEOPLE GROW APART AND FRIENDSHIPS END—AND THAT'S TOTALLY OKAY.

USE THIS SPACE TO WRITE A LETTER TO A PERSON YOU'RE UPSET WITH RIGHT NOW. EXPLAIN WHAT'S MAKING YOU SAD, ANGRY, OR CONFUSED. WRITING IT ALL OUT MIGHT HELP YOU FIGURE OUT WHAT YOU'RE FEELING AND HOW TO EXPRESS IT. OR MAYBE YOU'D PREFER TO DRAW IT OUT! IF SO, DRAW A REPRESENTATION OF THE SITUATION HERE.

_____

_____

_____

_____

_____

_____

_____

_____

_____

_____

_____

_____

_____

YOU CAN CHOOSE TO DELIVER THE LETTER OR JUST LEAVE IT HERE AS A RECORD OF YOUR FEELINGS. TOTALLY UP TO YOU!

USE THIS SPACE TO CREATE YOUR OWN DEFINITION OF FRIENDSHIP. WHAT MAKES A GOOD FRIEND? HOW ARE YOU A GOOD FRIEND TO YOUR FRIENDS?

FRIEND*SHIP (NOUN):

ONE THING THAT MAKES A GOOD FRIEND IS SUPPORTING SOMEONE WHEN THEY'RE GOING THROUGH A HARD TIME. HOW DO YOU SUPPORT YOUR FRIENDS IF THEY'RE UPSET OR GOING THROUGH SOMETHING SAD OR DIFFICULT? **THINK OF FIVE WAYS YOU CAN BE AN AWESOME FRIEND. LIST THEM BELOW.**

1 _____

_____

_____

_____

2

_____

3 _____

_____

_____

_____

4

_____

5 _____

_____

_____

ONE PROBLEM YOU AND YOUR FRIENDS MIGHT FACE IS BULLYING. KNOWING WHEN TO STAND UP FOR YOURSELF OR A FRIEND IS REALLY IMPORTANT. SOMETIMES YOU MAY EVEN KNOW YOUR BULLY, BUT SOMETIMES THEY CAN BE A TOTAL STRANGER! CYBERBULLYING IS ONE OF THE WAYS THAT NASTY PEOPLE USE THE INTERNET OR TECHNOLOGY TO MAKE OTHERS FEEL BAD ABOUT THEMSELVES.

WHAT ARE SOME WAYS YOU COULD HELP PROTECT YOURSELF AND YOUR FRIENDS FROM BULLYING?

DON'T BE AFRAID TO TELL AN ADULT AND ASK FOR HELP! ALSO, REMEMBER THAT YOU CAN ALWAYS UNPLUG FROM SOCIAL MEDIA FOR A LITTLE WHILE.

TRY TO BE A RAINBOW IN SOMEONE'S CLOUD

— MAYA ANGELOU

USE THIS SPACE TO WRITE A THANK-YOU NOTE TO A FRIEND—EITHER ONE WHO'S STILL IN YOUR LIFE OR WHO MAY NOT BE ANYMORE. WHAT DO YOU APPRECIATE ABOUT THAT FRIEND? FEEL FREE TO SHOW IT TO THEM OR KEEP IT TO YOURSELF!

TO: _____

FROM: _____

TWO TRUTHS & A LIE!

WRITE DOWN TWO TRUTHS AND ONE LIE ABOUT YOURSELF:

 1

 2

 3

HOW **HONEST** ARE YOU WITH YOUR FRIENDS? HOW IMPORTANT IS IT THAT YOUR FRIENDS ARE HONEST WITH YOU?

_____

_____

LIE TIME! WHICH STATEMENT WAS A LIE? ARE THERE LIES THAT YOU THINK ARE OKAY? EVEN IF THEY ARE FROM YOUR FRIENDS?

_____

_____

_____

_____

Quiz Time

WHAT KIND OF FRIENDSHIP IS MOST IMPORTANT TO YOU? ANSWER THE QUESTIONS BELOW TO FIND OUT!

HOW DO YOU EXPRESS YOURSELF AROUND YOUR FRIENDS? (THINK BACK TO THE SELF-EXPRESSION SECTION!)

A: I TELL THEM WHAT I'M THINKING AND HOW I FEEL ALL THE TIME.

B: I'M NOT AFRAID TO BE MY WEIRDEST SELF AROUND THEM.

C: I DON'T SHARE A LOT OF MY INNER THOUGHTS WITH MY FRIENDS.

WHEN YOUR FRIEND IS UPSET, WHAT DO YOU DO?

A: I GIVE THEM THE BEST ADVICE I CAN THINK OF.

B: I ASK THEM WHAT THEY NEED AND THEN MAKE SURE I DO IT.

C: I LISTEN TO THEM VENT OR CRY.

WHAT DO YOU APPRECIATE ABOUT YOUR FRIENDS?

A: THEY'RE CHATTERBOXES, JUST LIKE ME!

B: THEY LOVE ME FOR WHO I AM.

C: WE CAN BE QUIET TOGETHER AND DON'T ALWAYS HAVE TO TALK.

RESULTS:

MOSTLY As: YOU GRAVITATE TOWARD FRIENDS WHO ARE A LOT LIKE YOU—OUTGOING, OPINIONATED, AND HONEST!

MOSTLY Bs: YOU AND YOUR FRIENDS MAY ALL BE TOTALLY DIFFERENT, BUT THAT'S WHAT YOU LOVE ABOUT ONE ANOTHER AND YOUR FRIENDSHIP!

MOSTLY Cs: HAVING FRIENDS WHO WILL GIVE YOU SPACE WHEN YOU NEED IT IS IMPORTANT TO YOU (AND PROBABLY TO THEM)!

NO ONE CAN GET THROUGH LIFE WITHOUT A STRONG SQUAD BESIDE THEM. WHO ARE THE GO-TO PLAYERS ON YOUR ALL-STAR TEAM? **FILL IN THE NAMES OF YOUR FRIENDS AND FAMILY FOR EACH OF THE FOLLOWING SUPERLATIVES!**

(YOU CAN TOTALLY USE THE SAME PERSON MORE THAN ONCE!) YOU CAN EVEN ADD IN SOME FICTIONAL CHARACTERS, CELEBRITIES, OR WISH-LIST FRIENDS AS WELL.

BEST LISTENER

_____

MOST LIKELY TO MAKE YOU LAUGH SO HARD YOU CRY

_____

FASTEST TEXT ANSWERER

_____

BEST HUGGER

_____

MOST LIKELY TO GO VIRAL ON TIKTOK

_____

BEST ADVICE GIVER

_____

MOST LIKELY TO GET STRAIGHT As

_____

MOST HONEST

MOST LIKELY TO ADOPT A RESCUE PET

TRENDIEST DRESSER

BEST BEAUTY/MAKEUP GURU

BEST PERSON TO GO ON AN ADVENTURE WITH

MOST OPINIONATED

MOST LIKELY TO SCORE THE WINNING GOAL/POINT

BEST SHOULDER TO CRY ON

MOST LIKELY TO BE PRESIDENT

IMAGINE THAT YOU AND YOUR BESTIES ARE ALL REALLY, REALLY OLD. WHAT ARE YOU ALL DOING AND WHERE DO YOU LIVE? WHAT DOES YOUR FUTURE FRIENDSHIP LOOK LIKE? CAN YOU IMAGINE WAYS THAT YOU CAN STAY IN TOUCH IN THE FUTURE?

DRAW PICTURES OF YOU AND YOUR BFFS WHEN YOU'RE OLD AND GRAY HERE. DON'T FORGET THE WRINKLES (EACH ONE IS A SYMBOL OF SOME HAPPINESS YOU'VE EXPERIENCED IN BETWEEN NOW AND THEN)!

YOU AND YOUR BFF DON'T *NEED* AN EXTERNAL MARKER OF YOUR FRIENDSHIP, BUT **FRIENDSHIP BRACELETS** SURE ARE A FUN WAY TO CELEBRATE EACH OTHER. **COLOR IN THE BRACELETS BELOW TO DESIGN ALL KINDS OF DIFFERENT ONES FOR YOU AND YOUR FRIENDS.**

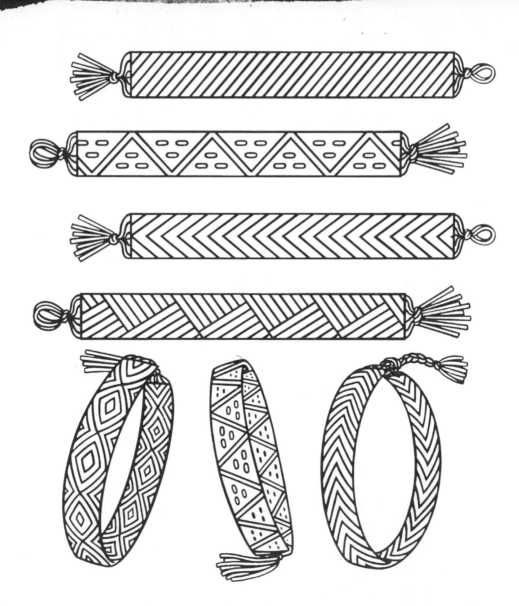

LET'S TALK ABOUT LOVE

A SPECIAL SOMEONE WHO MAKES YOU BLUSH!
DO YOU HAVE A CRUSH? WHAT DO YOU LIKE ABOUT THEM? USE SOME OF THE STICKERS TO SHOW HOW YOU FEEL!

DESCRIBE THEM AND WHY YOU LIKE THEM HERE—AND FEEL FREE TO LEAVE THEIR NAME OUT IF YOU WANT TO KEEP THAT INFO A SECRET FROM ANY SPYING EYES!

PS: IT'S OK IF YOU DON'T HAVE A CRUSH.

_____

_____

_____

_____

_____

_____

_____

WHETHER THIS IS YOUR FIRST CRUSH OR YOUR ONE HUNDREDTH, YOU MIGHT HAVE SOME QUESTIONS ABOUT WHAT IT MEANS TO HAVE A CRUSH AND HOW YOU SHOULD DEAL WITH IT. FOR EXAMPLE, WHEN SHOULD YOU MAKE A DECLARATION OF LIKE (IF YOU EVEN *WANT* TO DO THAT)?

WHAT ARE SOME QUESTIONS YOU HAVE ABOUT THE WORLD OF CRUSHING?

WHO ARE SOME PEOPLE YOU TRUST WHO YOU COULD GET SOME ANSWERS FROM? WHO WOULD HAVE ALL THE DETAILS ABOUT CRUSHES, LIKE, AND LOVE?

USE THIS SPACE TO DRAW A PORTRAIT—REALISTIC OR NOT—OF YOUR CURRENT OR A PAST CRUSH!

BE SURE TO INCLUDE SOME OF THE THINGS THEY LIKE—HOBBIES, PETS, CLASSES, ETC.—IN THE DRAWING. DO YOU AND YOUR CRUSH HAVE ANY OF THESE THINGS IN COMMON?

MAYBE YOUR ONE TRUE CRUSH IS YOURSELF!

THINK ABOUT YOUR FUTURE FAMILY AND DRAW ALL THE THINGS YOU WANT (OR DON'T WANT!).
PETS, KIDS, CARS, HOME, THE SKY'S THE LIMIT.

"IT'S ALWAYS WRONG TO HATE, BUT IT'S NEVER WRONG TO LOVE."

—LADY GAGA

PEER PRESSURE 101

AT TIMES, FRIENDS MAY WANT YOU TO DO SOMETHING THAT DOESN'T FEEL RIGHT. THIS MAY HAPPEN IN A GROUP SETTING OR JUST ONE ON ONE. IT'S IMPORTANT TO TRUST YOUR OWN INSTINCTS AND STICK TO WHAT MAKES YOU FEEL COMFORTABLE.

PEER PRESSURE IS WHEN SOMEONE OR A GROUP OF PEOPLE TRY TO INFLUENCE YOU TO DO SOMETHING THAT YOU MAY NOT BE COMFORTABLE WITH. REMEMBER, YOU CAN ALWAYS ASK AN ADULT OR GUARDIAN FOR HELP, TOO!

WHAT ARE SOME THINGS YOU COULD SAY TO EXPRESS YOUR FEELINGS IN A PEER-PRESSURE SITUATION?

FOR EXAMPLE: WHEN SOMEONE ASKS YOU TO GO SOMEWHERE AFTER SCHOOL THAT YOU KNOW IS OFF LIMITS—REPLY WITH: "NO THANKS, I HAVE TO HEAD HOME TO GUITAR PRACTICE."

_____

_____

_____

_____

_____

_____

"I'M **CONSTANTLY** IN A STATE OF **SELF-IMPROVEMENT,** BUT I DON'T BEAT MYSELF UP ABOUT IT."

—MINDY KALING

WHAT IS CONSENT?

GENERALLY, IT'S PERMISSION OR AN AGREEMENT FOR SOMETHING TO HAPPEN. IT'S AN IMPORTANT PART OF PERSONAL RELATIONSHIPS, WHETHER FRIENDSHIPS OR CRUSHES OR ANYTHING ELSE, AND IT'S DEFINITELY IMPORTANT IF YOU'RE THINKING ABOUT ANY KIND OF PHYSICAL INTERACTION. COMFORT IS KEY HERE. IF YOU AREN'T COMFORTABLE IN A GIVEN SITUATION OR INTERACTION, THEN IT PROBABLY ISN'T FOR YOU.

WHAT ARE SOME SITUATIONS IN WHICH CONSENT MAY COME UP BETWEEN TWO OR MORE PEOPLE?

ROSES ARE RED
VIOLETS ARE BLUE
A POEM IS A FUN WAY
TO TELL A CRUSH "I LIKE YOU!"

USE THIS SPACE TO DRAFT A **POEM** FOR YOUR CRUSH (YOU CAN KEEP IT HERE FOREVER OR GIVE IT TO THEM ONE DAY—IT'S TOTALLY UP TO YOU).

REMEMBER, IT DOESN'T HAVE TO RHYME!

_____

_____

_____

_____

_____

_____

_____

_____

_____

_____

_____

"IT'S HARD TO TELL PEOPLE HOW YOU REALLY, TRULY FEEL ABOUT THEM, ESPECIALLY IF THAT FEELING IS LOVE."

—LANA CONDOR

DO YOUR **CRUSH** AND YOUR FRIENDS GET ALONG? IF THEY DO, THAT'S GREAT! IF THEY DON'T, THAT'S OK, TOO, THOUGH IT MIGHT FEEL HARD TO DEAL WITH. EITHER WAY, YOU MIGHT WANT TO **BALANCE FRIEND TIME** WITH CRUSH TIME—IT'S ONLY FAIR! REMEMBER HOW IMPORTANT BALANCING THAT LIFE SEESAW IS?

FILL IN THE VENN DIAGRAM* BELOW WITH THINGS THAT FALL INTO THREE CATEGORIES: THINGS YOU DO WITH YOUR FRIENDS, THINGS YOU DO WITH YOUR CRUSH, AND THINGS YOU COULD DO WITH YOUR FRIENDS *AND* YOUR CRUSH:

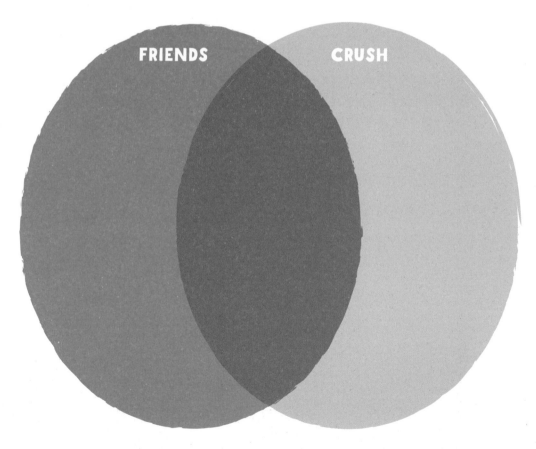

FRIENDS   CRUSH

*A VENN DIAGRAM IS A REALLY FUN WAY TO FIND OVERLAP BETWEEN ALL OF THE THINGS YOU ARE COMPARING.

Quiz Time

HOW DO YOU EXPRESS LOVE/LIKE? ANSWER THE QUESTIONS BELOW TO FIND OUT.

WHEN I HAVE A CRUSH, I . . .

A: SEND MY CRUSH SECRET-ADMIRER NOTES AND GIFTS.

B: BEFRIEND MY CRUSH BY JOINING AN ACTIVITY THAT WE'RE BOTH INTERESTED IN.

C: TRY TO COME UP WITH THE PERFECT WAY TO TELL MY CRUSH I LIKE THEM.

THE BEST WAY SOMEONE COULD SHOW ME THEY LIKE ME IS . . .

A: BUY ME THE PERFECT PRESENT FOR MY BIRTHDAY.

B: ASK ME TO HANG OUT, ONE-ON-ONE.

C: JUST TELL ME IN A STRAIGHTFORWARD WAY.

IF YOU COULD PICK ONE VALENTINE'S DAY GIFT, WHAT WOULD IT BE?

A: BOUQUET OF FLOWERS

B: FUN DATE

C: LOVE POEM WRITTEN BY MY CRUSH

RESULTS:

MOSTLY As: YOU LOVE TO EXPRESS YOUR LOVE (OR LIKE) THROUGH GIFTS AND OTHER THINGS THAT LET YOUR CRUSH KNOW YOU'RE THINKING OF THEM.

MOSTLY Bs: SPENDING QUALITY TIME WITH YOUR CRUSH IS THE MOST IMPORTANT THING TO YOU.

MOSTLY Cs: YOU WANT TO HEAR YOUR CRUSH TELL YOU THEY LIKE YOU, AND VICE VERSA!

MUSIC IS A GREAT WAY TO EXPRESS ALL KINDS OF FEELINGS! WHAT ARE YOUR FAVORITE LOVE SONGS?

IF YOU MADE **A PLAYLIST** FOR YOUR CRUSH,
WHAT SONGS WOULD BE ON IT?

LOOK UP SOME EPIC QUOTES ABOUT LOVE AND RECORD THEM HERE.

HOW DOES EACH ONE MAKE YOU FEEL? WHY DID YOU PICK EACH ONE? FEEL FREE TO DRAW A LITTLE SYMBOL NEXT TO EACH ONE TO REPRESENT THE QUOTE! HEARTS, STARS, EMOJI, AND EVERYTHING IN BETWEEN!

YOU MIGHT NOT HAVE A CRUSH RIGHT NOW, AND YOU MIGHT BE TOTALLY UNINTERESTED IN CRUSHES. THAT'S NORMAL! LOVE EXISTS IN SO MANY DIFFERENT WAYS—FAMILY LOVE, FRIEND LOVE, AND CRUSH LOVE. **WHAT ARE SOME THINGS IN YOUR LIFE THAT YOU'D RATHER SPEND YOUR ENERGY AND TIME ON?**

SOME EXAMPLES

* PERFECTING A NEW SKILL THROUGH LOTS OF PRACTICE
* SPENDING TIME WITH MY NON-CRUSH LOVED ONES
* READING A NEW AND EXCITING BOOK
*
*
*
*
*
*
*
*
*
*
*
*
*
*

DOODLE TIME!

DRAW SOMETHING THAT YOU LOVE; IT DOESN'T HAVE TO BE A PERSON!

ASSIGN A COLOR TO EVERY PERSON (OR ANIMAL) YOU LOVE IN YOUR LIFE. THEN FILL IN THIS PAGE WITH ALL THE COLORS, TO SYMBOLIZE ALL THE LOVE YOU HAVE AROUND YOU! YOU CAN ALTERNATE THE COLORS LIKE A RAINBOW, OR GO FOR A TIE-DYE EFFECT, OR DRAW FLOWERS WITH EACH COLOR TO CREATE A GARDEN OF LOVE.

HOROSCOPE

CAPRICORN
DECEMBER 22–JANUARY 19

AQUARIUS
JANUARY 20–FEBRUARY 18

PISCES
FEBRUARY 19–MARCH 20

ARIES
MARCH 21–APRIL 19

TAURUS
APRIL 20–MAY 20

GEMINI
MAY 21–JUNE 20

CANCER
JUNE 21–JULY 22

LEO
JULY 23–AUGUST 22

VIRGO
AUGUST 23–SEPTEMBER 22

LIBRA
SEPTEMBER 23–OCTOBER 22

SCORPIO
OCTOBER 23–NOVEMBER 21

SAGITTARIUS
NOVEMBER 22–DECEMBER 21

CHECK OUT THE TRAITS BELOW! DO YOU RECOGNIZE THESE TRAITS IN YOURSELF? DO YOU BELIEVE IN ASTROLOGY, THAT THE STARS AND THEIR POSITIONS IN THE SKY CAN INFLUENCE OUR PERSONALITIES AND LIVES?

EACH SIGN HAS ITS OWN SYMBOL THAT CORRESPONDS TO ITS STARS IN THE SKY. DRAW YOUR SIGN'S SYMBOL HERE!

CAPRICORN
INDEPENDENT, SERIOUS, DISCIPLINED

AQUARIUS
ORIGINAL, IMAGINATIVE, UNCOMPROMISING

PISCES
WISE, AFFECTIONATE, ARTISTIC

ARIES
COMPETITIVE, EAGER, DYNAMIC

TAURUS
CREATIVE, RELIABLE, STRONG

GEMINI
CURIOUS, KIND, EXPRESSIVE

CANCER
SENTIMENTAL, PROTECTIVE, COMPASSIONATE

LEO
OUTGOING, DRAMATIC, FIERY

VIRGO
LOYAL, GENTLE, PRACTICAL

LIBRA
FAIR, SOCIAL, GRACIOUS

SCORPIO
STUBBORN, PASSIONATE, BRAVE

SAGITTARIUS
FUNNY, GENEROUS, OPTIMISTIC

ASK YOUR FAMILY MEMBERS WHAT THEIR **ZODIAC SIGNS** ARE. LIST THEM HERE. HOW DO THE TRAITS OF YOUR SIGN AND THEIRS WORK TOGETHER?

_____

_____

_____

_____

_____

_____

_____

_____

_____

_____

_____

_____

_____

WHICH ZODIAC SIGNS ARE YOUR BFF'S? LIST THEM HERE.
HOW DO THE TRAITS OF YOUR SIGN AND THEIRS WORK TOGETHER?

CAPRICORN
_____
_____
_____
_____

AQUARIUS
_____
_____
_____
_____

PISCES
_____
_____
_____
_____

ARIES
_____
_____
_____

TAURUS
_____
_____
_____

GEMINI
_____
_____
_____

CANCER
_____
_____
_____
_____

LEO
_____
_____
_____
_____

VIRGO
_____
_____
_____
_____

LIBRA
_____
_____
_____
_____

SCORPIO
_____
_____
_____
_____

SAGITTARIUS
_____
_____
_____
_____

RESEARCH SOME **CELEBRITIES** WHO SHARE YOUR ZODIAC SIGN, AND EVEN
BETTER, YOUR ACTUAL BIRTHDAY! WHO ARE THEY? LIST SOME OF THEM HERE.

Taurus   Gemini   Cancer   Leo   Virgo   Capricorn

_____   _____
_____   _____
_____   _____
_____   _____
_____   _____
_____   _____
_____   _____
_____   _____
_____   _____
_____   _____
_____   _____
_____   _____
_____   _____

Aquarius   Pisces   Aries   Libra   Scorpio   Sagittarius

PICK A FEW FROM THE LIST AND MAKE UP A STORY ABOUT ALL OF YOU HANGING OUT. USE YOUR IMAGINATION—HOW WOULD YOU ALL GET ALONG, AND WHAT WOULD YOU DO TOGETHER? **NOW WRITE YOUR MASTERPIECE!**

A THEMED PLAYLIST!

THERE'S NOTHING AS FUN AS MAKING A THEMED PLAYLIST! WHAT SONGS WOULD BE ON YOUR ZODIAC THEMED PLAYLIST? THINK ABOUT THE TRAITS OF YOUR ZODIAC WHILE BRAINSTORMING SONG CHOICES.

Capricorn

Aquarius

Pisces

Aries

Taurus

Gemini

Cancer

Leo

Virgo

Libra

Scorpio

Sagittarius

WHY NOT TRY WRITING YOUR OWN SONG? **WRITE A SHORT SONG ABOUT YOU AND YOUR ZODIAC SIGN TRAITS. USE THIS SPACE TO WORKSHOP THE LYRICS AND RECRUIT THREE TO FIVE FRIENDS TO DO THE SAME.**

Quiz Time

HOW OBSESSED WITH THE ZODIAC ARE YOU? DO YOU LET THE STARS RUN YOUR LIFE? ANSWER THE QUESTIONS BELOW TO FIND OUT.

YOU READ YOUR HOROSCOPE . . .

A: EVERY DAY!

B: I CHECK IT SOMETIMES, BUT NOT ALL THE TIME

C: NEVER

YOU IDENTIFY WITH YOUR ZODIAC SIGN . . .

A: 110%

B: I DEFINITELY SEE SOME OF MY SIGN'S TRAITS IN MYSELF.

C: I DON'T IDENTIFY WITH MY SIGN AT ALL.

WHEN YOU MEET SOMEONE NEW, HOW MUCH DO YOU TALK ABOUT THE ZODIAC?

A: I IMMEDIATELY ASK THEM ABOUT THEIR BIRTH DATE AND SIGN.

B: I GET TO KNOW THEM FIRST, BUT USUALLY END UP ASKING ABOUT THEIR SIGN AT SOME POINT, JUST FOR FUN.

C: THE ZODIAC NEVER COMES UP UNLESS THEY BRING IT UP.

RESULTS:

MOSTLY As: THE ZODIAC RULES YOUR LIFE! REMEMBER THAT YOU'RE YOUR OWN PERSON, TOO!

MOSTLY Bs: YOU DABBLE WITH THE ZODIAC, BUT YOU'RE NOT OBSESSED.

MOSTLY Cs: YOU ARE YOUR OWN BOSS, AND THERE'S NO SUCH THING AS "WRITTEN IN THE STARS" AS FAR AS YOU'RE CONCERNED!

NEED SOME YOU TIME? TAKE A MOMENT TO RELAX
AND COLOR IN THE ICONS BELOW!

_____

_____

_____

_____

_____

_____

_____

_____

_____

_____

_____

_____

_____

_____

NOW THAT THIS BOOK IS COMING TO AN END, IT'S TIME TO CHECK IN WITH YOURSELF. **USE THIS SPACE TO WRITE A NOTE TO YOUR FUTURE SELF**—WHAT HAVE YOU LEARNED ABOUT YOURSELF AND THE WORLD BY FILLING OUT THIS BOOK? WHAT DO YOU HOPE TO KEEP WITH YOU AND REMEMBER? WHEN WILL YOU COME BACK AND READ THIS FUTURE-YOU NOTE?